A Small Dog's Big Life

Around the World with Owney

Irene Kelly

Holiday House / New York

For Nellie, Ruby, Pogo, Pearl, and Izzy . . .
and adventurous dogs everywhere.

Special thanks to my agent, Edite Kroll,
my editor, Mary Cash, art director Claire
Counihan, and the librarians
at the National Postal Museum in
Washington, D.C.

And love and gratitude to Jeffrey, Derek,
and Lucy . . . my small life is much bigger
thanks to you.

Text and illustrations copyright © 2005 by Irene Kelly
Maps on pages 8–9 and pages 24–25 by Heather Saunders.
Maps copyright © 2005 by Holiday House, Inc.
All Rights Reserved
Printed in the United States of America
www.holidayhouse.com
First Edition
1 3 5 7 9 10 8 6 4 2

Library of Congress Cataloging-in-Publication Data
Kelly, Irene.
A small dog's big life: around the world with Owney / Irene Kelly. —1st ed.
p. cm.
Summary: Letters tell the story of Owney, a dog who became the mascot of the Albany, New York,
post office in 1888 and traveled around the world. Includes historical notes.
ISBN 0-8234-1863-4 (hardcover)
1. Owney (Dog)—Juvenile fiction. [1. Owney (Dog)—Fiction. 2. Dogs—Fiction. 3. Postal service—Fiction.
4. Mascots—Fiction. 5. Letters—Fiction.] I. Title.
PZ10.3.K295Sm 2005
[E]—dc22
2004047507

THE ALBANY RECORD

ALBANY, NEW YORK   NOVEMBER 19, 1889

Albany, New York—Who is the new fellow in the post office? You know the one I mean, he's exceedingly short and in desperate need of a shave. With the notable exception of cats and squirrels, his personality overflows with goodwill toward everyone he meets. By all accounts, he lives in the post office day and night, accepting leftover scraps of food and humbly sleeping on an empty mail sack behind the counter. Where did he come from? Will he be staying for long or will he move on? These are the questions this reporter set out to answer. . . .

December 11, 1889

Mr. John Wannamaker
Postmaster General
Washington, D.C.

Dear Mr. Wannamaker,
Meet Owney! When he wandered into our post office a few weeks ago he was cold, hungry, and homeless. Today he is beloved by every postal clerk and has more food and attention than he ever dreamed possible. He is very affectionate and as bright as a button, though I must admit a bit scruffy (even after several good soakings).

It isn't just the clerks who are fond of Owney. It's the general population of Albany! Since Owney's arrival, people have been visiting our post office in record numbers, some coming in just to cuddle and play with him.

Owney is well suited to the busy life of the post office. He enjoys greeting all who enter while keeping a watchful eye on the mailbags. This may sound strange, but he is devoted to the mailbags. He follows them around all day long, and at night he leaps onto the highest bag and makes himself a cozy bed.

Today we gave Owney a collar with a tag that reads: "Owney, Post Office, Albany, New York" with the hope that if he ever gets lost, he'll be quickly returned to us. While attaching this collar to Owney, I realized that we never got official permission for him to live here.

I don't know of a rule that forbids a dog from living in a post office but we are checking with you, just in case. We have our fingers (and paws) crossed that you will agree to Owney staying on with us here in Albany.

Yours respectfully,
Owen Smith
Postal Clerk
Albany, New York

P.S. Lately, Owney has been riding with the mailbags on the wagon to the train station. I wouldn't be surprised if one day he jumps right into a mail car!

January 12, 1890

To: Mr. Owen Smith
    Albany, New York

    As you thought he might, Owney jumped aboard
our train this morning (the 9:46 for New York City).
I've been watching him think about taking the leap
for several days and am glad he finally worked up
the courage to do it.

    Owney greeted each of us with the funny little
sneezes that are his unique way of saying HELLO!
Soon he settled onto a mail sack by the open
freight car door in a perfect position to appreciate
the sights and smells of the passing countryside.
Owney bolted up whenever we made a stop along the
way, but he made no move to jump off the train till
we pulled into New York City. At that point Owney
quickly scampered into the station, where the city
postal workers gave him a warm welcome. They knew
exactly who he was because of the newspaper stories
about the "post office mascot in Albany."

    I left Owney in their hands. As we pulled out
of the station, I saw someone hand Owney a sandwich
out of his lunch box. The clerks were debating over
who would have the pleasure of taking Owney on a
grand tour of the city!

                    Sincerely,
                    Jeffrey Bernard
                    Railroad Mail Clerk

February 19, 1890

To Postal Clerks of Albany,

Your pooch, Owney, is in New York City! What a sight he was when he raced into our mail depot at Pennsylvania Station: those two curious eyes, those four spindly legs, and that straggly (but waggly) tail. Since the clerks from Albany asked to be kept informed as to the little dog's whereabouts, here is your first bulletin:

I'm happy to report that New York City will never be the same: Owney has won everyone's heart! He has spent the last week walking the beat with our mail carriers. He has hiked the entire length of Broadway and crossed the Brooklyn Bridge several times. He even visited the Statue of Liberty, where he was quite an attraction himself.

I attempted to send him back to Albany today, but Owney had other plans. He darted across the middle tracks to the westbound trains and bounded onto the 9:05 for Chicago, Illinois. It seems that he has more traveling to do before he heads back home.

Most sincerely,
Derek Kelly
Post Office
New York, New York

P.S. Owney has developed a taste for a real New York City specialty . . . bagels with cream cheese. Ever hear of that in Albany?

P.P.S. We have fixed a tag onto Owney's collar to commemorate his visit to New York City. We've also added a note asking that other clerks who meet Owney along his travels do the same. Soon he'll have so many tags that their jingling and jangling will let every-one know when he's approaching!

The Herald

NEW YORK, NEW YORK JULY 2, 1890

OWNEY, BELOVED POSTAL POOCH, TRAVELS FROM COAST TO COAST

Devoted fans turn out by the hundreds to greet Owney wherever he goes, which is everywhere in this great country of ours. His travels have taken this curious canine to nearly every state in the Union, and he's still young! Who knows, perhaps he'll even venture beyond our borders. . . .

July 14, 1890

Postal Clerks
Albany Post Office
Albany, New York
United States

To Whom It May Concern:
"Owney" has crossed the U.S.-Canada border illegally.
He is now under detention in Montreal, Canada. Since the dog
entered the country without a license or proper identifica-
tion papers, you are hereby fined $2.50. By law the animal
must remain locked up until payment has been received.
Once the fine is paid, Owney will be released to an
American postal worker who will escort him out of Canada.

Steven Allendorf
Animal Warden
Montreal, Canada

P.S. I haven't had a moment's peace since Owney's arrival
and especially now that he's taken to howling at the moon! I
would appreciate payment as swiftly as possible.

August 23, 1892

Postal Clerks
Albany, New York

Dear Clerks,

For the past few years I've been following the newspaper accounts of Owney's travels. I've always hoped that one day your adventurous dog would show up in Boston. Well, he finally arrived here last week. He seemed tired and in need of some fresh air. It was clear to me that he would benefit from a vacation. My family agreed wholeheartedly, so we grabbed our tent and headed for the ocean.

At first everything was just as I'd hoped. Owney dashed along the beach, plunged into the waves, and chased crabs and sandpipers. But by the evening of the second day, he seemed restless. It is plain to me now that he was planning something, though at the time I could never have guessed what was about to happen.

When we woke up the next morning, Owney was gone! It turns out that Owney hightailed it for the piers and boarded the first boat back to Boston! Upon his arrival in Boston Harbor, Owney raced to the Old Colony Railroad Station, where he jumped aboard the 8:50 out of town.

I have never met anyone—man, woman, or dog—who loved trains more than Owney. What an astonishing animal.

Sincerely,
Lillie M. Donohue
Postal Clerk
Boston, Mass.

P.S. Are you aware of the tags Owney is carrying around on his collar? It seems that everywhere he goes, the postal clerks make him a tag as a "souvenir" of his visit. But the weight of all these tags is making it hard for Owney to lift his head. I have removed them and am sending them on to you, as they will make a good record of Owney's travels.

June 2, 1895

To: Postal Clerks
    Albany, New York

¡Hola, Albany!

Señor Owney is with us in Mexico! We have taken him high up into the mountains and across the desert. He is very brave and a little reckless. Owney has an interest in snakes. He stalks them and then pounces, but has not succeeded in catching one . . . yet. Lucky for him, as many of our snakes have a poisonous bite that can be deadly.

Owney is also fascinated by cactus. On one occasion he got too close to the thorns, and he let out a yelp that must have been heard north of the border!

Owney has made many amigos here, and we will miss him when he departs on his big voyage. We have heard that he is soon to go to Washington State, where he is to begin a journey that will take him all the way around the world! I suppose it's only fair that we share Owney with the citizens of every country. We will follow his adventures in the newspaper and hope that one day he will return to Mexico.

Adiós,
Señor Rodriguez
Mexico City, Mexico

August 11, 1895

Mr. Smith
Postal Clerk
Albany, New York

Dear Mr. Smith:

In accordance with the arrangements we made, Owney has arrived here in Tacoma, Washington, safely and will soon leave on his voyage to Japan. He will, no doubt, be the first dog to travel around the world. I'm honored that he is to begin his voyage aboard the steamship Victoria. He arrived with a tiny suitcase attached to his harness, a gift from Postmaster General Wannamaker, I understand. In it were a blanket, a comb, and a brush. It's quite a novelty to have a dog on board (much less one with his own suitcase).

Owney has already chosen a favorite mailbag to use as a bed. It is located just behind the galley (that's the kitchen), which is definitely his favorite room. He wasted no time getting to know the cook and has already made clear his preference for beef jerky, which we happen to have by the barrelful. I will write again once we have docked in Yokohama, Japan.

Cordially,
William Grant, Captain
The Victoria

P.S. Owney doesn't neatly fit into any standard mail category, so we created one especially for him. He is traveling as a "Registered Dog Package."

October 2, 1895

Mr. Smith
Postal Clerk
Albany, New York

Dear Mr. Smith:

Now I've seen everything! An official was sent by the emperor to welcome Owney to Japan! He was even given an Imperial Passport, which allows him to explore the country, as long as he obeys the following rules:

He may not:

- rent a house
- attend fires on horseback
- scribble on buildings
- hire a carriage without headlamps at night

"No problem," I assured the emperor's aide. "Owney is a law-abiding dog." I declined to mention that little problem in Canada. Owney is having a swell time in Japan.

Sayonara,

William Grant, Captain
The <u>Victoria</u>

P.S. I've finally discovered something that Owney WON'T eat . . . sushi (raw fish). It's not as bad as it sounds. In fact, I always miss it when I return to the U.S.

SHANGHAI POSTCARD

October 20, 1895

To: Albany Clerks

I am most happy to report that Owney has learned to navigate our city's twisty streets with great success. Shanghai has a wall around its perimeter, so we need never worry about losing him! Today he leaves for Hong Kong, where the newspapers have been tracking his progress. Many citizens are sure to be on the dock, ready to welcome this daring world traveler.

Jing Weng
Postal Clerk

POSTCARD

Hong Kong
October 29, 1895

To: Clerks
Albany Post Office
Albany, New York
U.S.A.

We have shown Owney around Hong Kong Island. His favorite way to travel is by rickshaw, although he has the worrisome habit of jumping off of it. He loves chasing monkeys but he hasn't caught one yet, and I don't think he'd know what to do if he did. He is on his way to Singapore tomorrow.

Kyung-Shen

CARTE POSTALE EGYPTIENNE

Port Said, Egypt
November 9, 1895

To: Postal Clerks
Albany, New York
U.S.A.

We have been delighted to have Owney as our guest here in Egypt. He has seen the pyramids, the Great Sphinx, and many camels. But his biggest treat came last Friday when his boat took him through the new Suez Canal. Next, he'll go to Algiers, North Africa. I understand that Owney will trot back to his ship, the <u>Port Phillip</u>, on November 30th and begin his voyage home. The people of Egypt would welcome our furry American friend back anytime.

Owney is doing well on his journey around the globe. He is full of curiosity and affection, and is as popular in Egypt as he is everywhere he goes.

Akil Zer

The Herald

OWNEY CONQUERS THE WORLD

Owney, the famous mascot of the United States Postal Service, has almost completed his journey around the world! He left Tacoma, Washington, on August 19, 1895, on the steamship *Victoria*. First stop, Yokohama, Japan! He then stopped in China to visit Shanghai, Woosung, Foochow, and Hong Kong. From there his voyage took him southward, through the South China Sea to Singapore. Then he ventured through the Suez Canal, stopped briefly in Port Said, Egypt, and on to Algiers, North Africa. His last stop was the Azore Islands in the North Atlantic Ocean. As you read this, Owney is aboard the *Port Phillip*, steaming back to New York, where hundreds of well-wishers will be on hand to welcome him home.

GREEN

ALASKA

CANADA

Vancouver

Winnepeg

Montreal

Tacoma

Boston

New York

UNITED STATES

A

MEXICO

Atlantic

Mexico City

Oce

Pacific

Ocean

SOUTH
AMERICA

Owney's Voyage ....

December 24, 1895

Mr. Owen Smith
Post Office
Albany, New York

Dear Mr. Smith:

Merry Christmas! We have just docked in New York City and put Owney on a train headed west to Tacoma, Washington. That way he can end his round-the-world tour where he started. He will arrive there in 5 days, so it will have taken him 132 days to voyage around the world, which I imagine is a record for a dog. Nellie Bly, the American journalist, managed to do it in 1890 in just 72 days, 6 hours, and 11 minutes, but she was at liberty to plan out her train schedules whereas Owney had to catch as catch can.

Owney was a great addition to the crew during the voyage home. He chased down more rats than any cat I've ever had on board! I'll miss his hunting abilities as well as his habit of sneezing to say hello. I'll miss seeing the way he insisted on wriggling back into his harness whenever we tried to remove it. Most of all, I'll miss his companionship.

Owney has put on 6 pounds, and he seems quite weary of traveling. I've been wondering if it's time for him to retire. I'm sure you are eager to see him, so I have sent instructions to the clerks in Tacoma to place Owney on the first train for Albany after officially completing his record-setting voyage. Maybe then he can put up his paws for a while.

Sincerely,
Charles Grey, Captain
The <u>Port Phillip</u>

May 16, 1896

Mr. John Wannamaker
Post Master General
Washington, D.C.

Dear Mr. Wannamaker,
I am writing to inform you of Owney's retirement. As you know, Owney has been riding the postal trains for the last 7 years.
Clerks all over America will miss sliding open the mail car doors and greeting their loyal friend. Over the years they've come to regard Owney as a good-luck charm, since there has never been an accident on any train carrying him (very impressive, given how frequent derailments, collisions, and explosions are these days). Some clerks are convinced that Owney can tell time and that he understands the meanings of all the engine whistles and bells. I, for one, believe it. Nothing about Owney ever surprises me.
According to our information, Owney has traveled about 143,000 miles and collected more than 1,017 tags from all over the U.S.! He has also won many medals and awards at dog shows throughout the country. Owney is certainly due his rest, and lately he's been spending a lot of time snoozing on the mailbags. It looks as if Owney's travels are finally over.

Yours most respectfully,
Owen Smith
Postal Clerk
Albany, New York

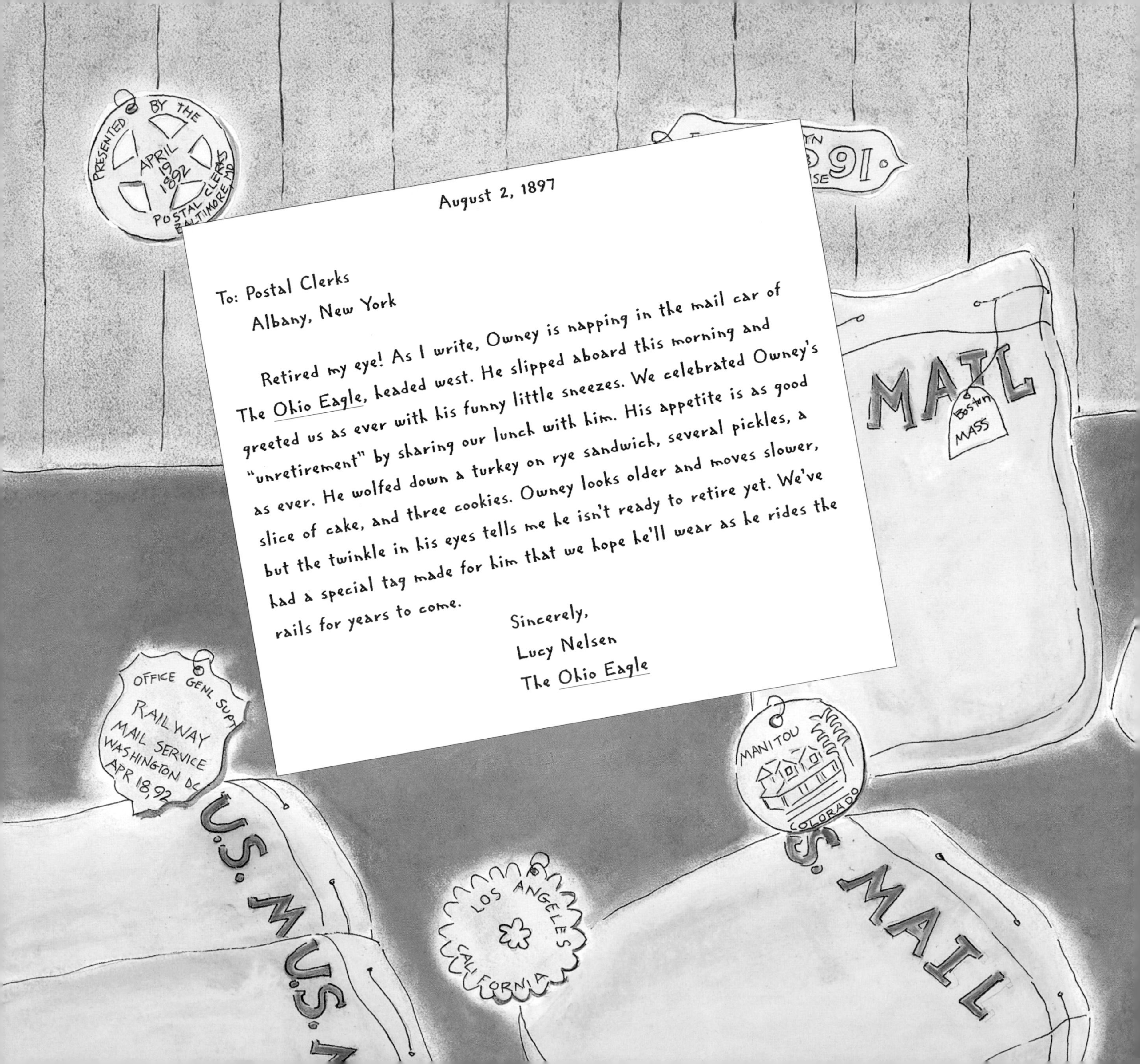

August 2, 1897

To: Postal Clerks
Albany, New York

Retired my eye! As I write, Owney is napping in the mail car of The Ohio Eagle, headed west. He slipped aboard this morning and greeted us as ever with his funny little sneezes. We celebrated Owney's "unretirement" by sharing our lunch with him. His appetite is as good as ever. He wolfed down a turkey on rye sandwich, several pickles, a slice of cake, and three cookies. Owney looks older and moves slower, but the twinkle in his eyes tells me he isn't ready to retire yet. We've had a special tag made for him that we hope he'll wear as he rides the rails for years to come.

Sincerely,
Lucy Nelsen
The Ohio Eagle

Author's Note

A *Small Dog's Big Life* is the true story of a dog named Owney that lived more than one hundred years ago. Since Owney really did live with postal workers, I thought it would be fun to tell his story in an epistolary form—that's a story told entirely in letters. I invented the letters, postcards, and newspaper clippings in this book, but they are based on fact.

The tags, on the other hand, are real! Clerks from all over the United States really did have special tags made for Owney to commemorate his visit to their towns. The tags are now in an exhibit at the National Postal Museum, which is part of the Smithsonian Institute in Washington, D.C.

In 1896 the Albany clerks thought that Owney was getting too old to travel and should retire. Owney had other ideas. In June of the next year, he snuck out of the Albany post office and jumped aboard a mail train headed for Toledo, Ohio. It isn't clear what happened next, but it seems that a postal worker handled Owney roughly while showing him off to a newspaper reporter. Owney bit the offending postal worker and the following day a police officer came to the post office and removed Owney. Owney was put down as a dangerous animal on June 11, 1897. He is thought to have been about seventeen years old. There was an angry outcry from people all over the country when the news of Owney's death was reported in the papers. Many postal workers said that Owney couldn't have hurt anyone since he had lost all of his teeth by 1897!

James E. White, superintendent of the Railway Mail Service, collected money from many postal clerks to have a taxidermist preserve Owney. Thanks to Mr. White, today you can see Owney in the National Postal Museum, where he has a place of honor in the atrium.

Although a lot is known about Owney's travels, such as where he went and when he traveled, we know little about exactly what he did in the places he visited. Did he climb the Statue of Liberty while he was in New York City? There's no record of it, but I like to imagine that some postal clerk took him to see one of the city's most popular attractions. Did he actually ride in a rickshaw when he was in Shanghai? Nobody knows, but since he loved trains, I'm sure he would have enjoyed a nice rickshaw ride, so that's how I portrayed him during his visit to China.

In telling Owney's story, I've relied on the facts as much as possible, but I've also taken some liberties and imagined things he might have done or seen. Given his adventurous spirit, I'm sure he would have loved yapping at the seagulls on Lady Liberty's crown

I had lots of fun working on this book. I spent many afternoons finding out where Owney actually went, how he got there, what he ate, and more. Although I found the answers to many of my questions, I didn't find the answer to one: Where did Owney get his unusual name? No one knows for sure, but there are two good possibilities:

Owney often walked with a mail carrier named Eugene Wise, whose nickname was Owen. Maybe Owney got his name through that friendship.

Another possibility is that since Owney had no home or family when he entered the Albany post office, the clerks must have wondered if anyone owned him. "Who's your owner?" they might have asked. Maybe the name Owney came from that question being asked over and over again.

What do you think?